MW00892549

Manhattan Max
A City Dog

Mary Andrea Anderson

Mary Anderson

To my mother and dad,
Bernyce and Bill Lemke
R.I.P.

Acknowledgments

I would like to thank:

A special thanks to Mellissa and Brad McCullough for allowing me to paint their beautiful children, Alley and Wyatt. I knew from the first moment I saw her that she was my Billy.

Patricia Gerdeman-Moellman, who nagged me all through school to write my stories down, and for a lifetime of friendship. You are forever in my heart.

Zack Hall, my biggest cheerleader, for believing I was amazing and could do anything, even write and paint books. I hear you every day.

Amanda Harper, for being there from the very beginning.

Tim Aiken, Aiken Industries

Cynthia Wright Photography

My family, for your continued support, especially, Lilyana Grace Hanley, who always gives me the invaluable thumbs-up or thumbs-down.

CONTENTS

1

CITY LIFE

It was a great morning for Maximilian T. McKnight, otherwise known as Manhattan Max, or just Max to his very special friends. He was full of energy and bursting with excitement because he was convinced that today was the day Ma and Pa were finally coming home. While it was hard for him to admit, he had missed them very much. In fact, he had been down in the dirt, downright lonesome. *I sure don't know why they couldn't take me along, like always. I think I'll sulk for a whole day when they finally get here!* He promised himself.

Max tried to pass the time with Zsa Zsa, the poodle dog who lived on the fifth floor. Although she had pretty white fur and long lashes, she was, after all, just a girl. Max did not have much time for girlie, girls, except Ma, of course. Ma was different. She could ride a bike, run, hunt and throw duck decoys, just like Pa.

Max loved living with Ma and Pa in the condominium up in the sky. He could bask in the sun on the roof, ride up and down on the elevator, and greet all of Ma's guests at the front door. Mostly, he loved the city life. Maximilian T. McKnight was a city dog and proud of it. He got haircuts and pedicures at the finest spa, wore a plaid cap like Pa, and a jewel-stud collar with gold chains around his neck. Some might say he was a little stuck up, but Max just secretly knew he was a superior dog. He was, after all, a giant, black Schnauzer (sounds like Shh-now-zer), and a descendant of an impressive family of show dogs. Ma always told him, "Max, you are the best looking bachelor in the whole city." Max, of course, wholeheartedly agreed.

There were many telling signs that this was going to be a very special day. There was a flurry going on all over the house. Great aunt Sophie, his temporary caretaker, was cleaning, cooking, and setting the table, all at the same time. There were fresh flowers everywhere and she was making faces at Max that meant he better stay out of her way.

Staying home with Sophie had been a real hardship. There was no eating between meals or long walks along the river. In fact, things had not been the same since she discovered his favorite catfish, resting peacefully under her bed.

Max did not waste any time escaping to the roof where Pa's version of a doggie hammock was his favorite place for an afternoon nap. It was just low enough so he could step in one paw at a time.

He could lay on his back, sway back and forth, and snooze the day away, just like Pa.

It was already dark by the time Max woke up. *Hmm, I timed that just right. I'll fly down the stairs, jump in the bed, and slobber kisses all over them. I'll bet they're sorry now that they didn't take me along.*

Max crept into the bedroom and stared intently at the bed. He placed his nose on the side of the bed so he could get a closer look. Within a second, he jumped back and shook himself all over.

Yikes! Two big size heads, one medium, and one small head peeking out? That means two grownup people and two kids, the little people who spill stuff and make a mess all over. One of them is even wearing Ma's pink shirt! Wonder what I should do. They're definitely imposters, up to no good. I better lie down in my thinking position and figure it all out. Yep, that's what I'll do.

Max stretched his front legs out as far as he could, tucked his head down inside and covered his ears.

Maybe I should try to look on the bright side. There's probably a really good explanation for why these strangers are in the house. After all, Sophie doesn't seem worried. She's not making faces at me or anything. I'll just go to sleep and everything will be better in the morning.

While there were still no slobbering kisses from Ma and Pa the next morning, he did receive a few head pats from the pink shirt kid.

It didn't take long, however, for him to realize what the strangers were up to. Max started barking. "Hey, what are you doing rummaging through all the drawers and packing up everything? Hurry, Sophie, call the police," he pleaded. "They're a gang of robbers. Look, now they're taking all the furniture. Maybe they're going to take you, too!"

When Max found Sophie at the front door, she was talking with several men dressed in overalls, with heavy black belts. He continued to frantically, bark and pace around her, but she paid no attention. It didn't take long, however, until the pink shirt kid came back. He patted and consoled Max until he was quiet and stayed down.

After he left, Max began to think about the kid in Ma's pink shirt.

Maybe the kid isn't one of them. A thief wouldn't wear Ma's pink shirt, unless, it's a girl. No, no, it's a boy kid. He walks like a boy, talks like a boy, doesn't squeal and giggle; it's a boy. I think he wants to help me and I'll try to get him to help Sophie, too.

Max stayed in place waiting for the kid to come back, but once the men carried his bed and food dish out the door, there was no more waiting. *This is it! I've got to get out before they haul me off, too. Ruining my lifestyle is one thing, but stealing, that's something else again.*

2

FAREWELL

It was dark when Maximilian T. McKnight managed to escape through the giant sliding doors and out to the street. They didn't call him Manhattan Max for nothing. He maneuvered his way around tall buildings, through crowds, and heavy traffic. When he could break free, he raced toward the river.

"Hey, stop! Where ya going so fast, anyhow? You almost ran me over."

Even with the wind in his ears, Max knew it was the big

bark of a very little dog, his best pal, Mickey.

"I've been looking for you, there's an emergency! We've gotta get to the river, quick." Max called back.

"You bet! Race ya to the bridge," Mickey challenged. Compared to Max who weighed over 90 pounds, Mickey weighed-in at less than 20 pounds, and was only 12 inches tall.

They were great friends. No one ever dared to call him "weenie" or "wiener" dog when Max was around. After all, Mickey was a world-renowned, champion Dachshund (sounds like Docks-und or Doxin). Despite his short, little legs, he could run up to 20 mph in a short race and was the father of lots and lots of puppies.

Max waited for Mickey, so they could reach the bridge together. Bo Beagle, Rex Retriever, Benny Boxer, and the three girls, Lily Labrador, Penny the Copper Cocker, and Zsa Zsa, were all there. They all yapped and barked, as Max and Mickey shared the news.

"Haven't you ever moved before?" Bo Beagle asked. "No, I've lived here for as long as I can remember," Max answered.

Pacing back and forth, Lily Labrador said, "I think Bo is right. Sounds to me like your peeps are moving to a different house."

"What if the house is far away? How will I ever see Max again?" Zsa Zsa whined. Mickey strolled over until he was eye to eye with Zsa Zsa. "You'll just have to marry me, ha, ha," he yapped at her.

Max made a big woof, "You guys are just the right size for each other. I'll even give you my hammock for a wedding present. Well, if it's still there, that is."

Rex Retriever and Benny Boxer looked sadly at their friend. "We don't want you to go but you should probably hurry home. What if they go and leave without you?" 'Where will you sleep and get fed? If you end up homeless, we will feel even worse than we do right now."

Sadly, Max looked out at the circle of friends that were gathered around him. "I guess you're all probably right. Maybe I did jump to conclusions. No matter how long it takes, I better go back and wait for Ma and Pa, and probably look after the kids, too. I'll be seeing you."

Lily Labrador, put her nose next to Max. "Goodbye, Manhattan, I'll never forget you."

"You're alright, too, Lily," Max replied, sweetly. Then, he turned, and staring straight ahead, he slowly walked away.

"Goodbye, Manhattan Max, city dog," they barked all together.

3

THE CHASE

When Max reached the house, all the strangers were gathered in the living room. Each one had a rug and they were sleeping on the floor. He walked through the house and saw that all the rooms were empty. Then he bent down and sniffed each one of the strangers until he got to the one that smelled the best. *Here he is and he's got an extra rug, too. I wonder if he's saving it for me.* Max lay down beside the kid who had finally given up Ma's pink shirt for a pair of jeans, a t-shirt, and black, high-top sneakers.

I just knew it was a boy kid. What a relief, he sighed and fell sound asleep. Just before dawn, Max woke up to a noise that instantly, brought him to his feet. He listened intently, then, nudged the boy with his paws to wake him up. "What's up, Max? Do you need to go out?" the boy asked. He barely had time to hook the leash before Max bolted toward the door.

The boy struggled to keep Max quiet, as they rode down

the elevator to the ground floor. When the doors opened, Max stood very still and listened one more time. He would know that whistle anywhere. He jerked his leash free, made his way across the street, and there was Pa; and just a few feet away, there was Ma, on her knees with her arms out, waiting for Max. They wrestled with Max on the grass, ruffled his ears and chased him around the park.

Ma and Pa made sure he understood that everything was all right and they were sorry they were gone for so long. *This is the best day ever, Pa, Ma, and Max together again. We will get all the furniture back, go up on the roof and cook, and Pa and I can snooze in our hammocks together.*

As usual, it wasn't long before Max's daydream ended and he was up, jumping and barking again. "Look, Ma, Pa! The strangers are getting away in that truck and they've got Sophie and the baby kid, too."

Max became more confused than ever. Despite all his efforts, Ma and Pa were too busy hugging and squeezing the boy to notice anything he did. When Pa finally paid attention to Max, he quickly, fastened the leash around his neck and led him into the back of the car. Then, he led the boy into the car, right next to Max. *Pa must have saved him from the rest of the strangers,* Max thought as he tried to analyze the situation.

As happy as he was that the boy was safe, Max lay down and covered his ears. He couldn't stop worrying about Sophie and the other little kid, all alone in a truck full of strangers.

When Pa noticed Max had covered his ears, he knew right away he was distressed. "Cheer up, Max. You are going to love it where we're going. I'll play some good country music, how about that? It'll be just like old times," Pa told him.

After many days on the road, Pa pulled over and let Max run free in acres of green grass. When Pa whistled him back, he and Ma led Max into a low, wide house, next to a grove of trees. It didn't have a rooftop patio, stairs or elevators, but what it did have was Sophie, the smaller, little kid, and the other strangers.

Max stared in amazement, as Pa introduced everyone. "Max, this is our daughter and son-in-law, and our two grandchildren, Billy and little Wyatt. They are your family, too, and this is your new home. Family, meet Max, better known as Manhattan Max."

"Come on, Max, how about some supper," Sophie called from the kitchen. Max didn't hesitate when he heard the word supper. "How are you, old friend, have you missed me?" Sophie asked. Max shook himself and licked her nose. He sat up, at attention, and waited for Sophie's specialty, dog food, with bacon bits and hamburger sprinkles on the top.

It didn't take long for Max to get used to his new surroundings. He still missed his social life down by the river, but rolling in the grass and chasing the kids kept him pretty busy. One night after supper, Pa took Max out for a long walk and one of his heart-to-heart talks.

There's nothing better than going out with Pa. I bet we're going to the river. I can smell the catfish now, Max imagined.

Pa did not head for the river that night. He turned onto the road and stopped at a big sign, close to the corner. "This is the bus stop where the kids catch the school bus. I've got an important job for you, Max. I want you to start walking Billy to the bus stop and back home every day," Pa told him. "I'll walk with you until you know your way. Then how about we head out to the new fishing hole? What do you think about that? Remember, Max, if you ever lose your way, always follow the river just like you did back home."

Several weeks after school started and Max had completed his training, he took his usual position by the bus steps. He sniffed and looked over every child as they got off the bus. When he did not see Billy, he ran around the bus, searching in every direction. Just as the bus doors began to close, Max jumped onto the bus. "Hey, you, you can't come on here. This is for kids, not for big dogs like you," the bus driver hollered.

Max twisted and turned, looking on the floor and behind the seats, until the man got behind him and pushed him out the door. Before he could figure out what to do next, the bus took off and Max tore down the road after it. He had only one thing on his mind. He must find his new friend, who had become just as important to him as Ma and Pa.

4

THE PINK SHIRT KID

Max ran after the bus until it was long out of sight. When his legs finally gave out, he slowed down to a slow walk, then a limp, and finally, he crawled to the side of the road on his belly. He only had time to lick one sore paw before he felt the hairs prickling on the back of his neck. Sensing he was no longer alone, Max turned and saw a very odd-looking creature lying on the ground behind him. *Yikes, I've never seen anything like that before. It might be dead. I better check it out.*

Max stood up and glared down at the creature. "Don't just lay there and pretend you're dead. I saw you move. So, you may as well open your eyes and tell me who you are. No, better yet, tell me what you are," Max demanded.

It's not answering. Maybe it really is dead. It sure doesn't look like any mice or rats that I've ever seen.

Suddenly the creature hissed and showed its sharp teeth. "Hey, you, up there, you better watch your step. I could scratch you up in a New York minute," it said.

Max locked eyes with the creature and took a half step back. "Don't make fun of my town. I may be Manhattan Max, a city dog, but I'm sure, not afraid of something that has no hair on its tail and lies around pretending to be dead. So, let's get over it and move on. I've come a long way. I'm hungry and I need a nap."

"Okay, okay," the creature replied. "Just keep those giant paws to yourself. I am Mr. Oliver O. Possum, but my friends call me Mr. O. Don't just call me Possum because none of them live around here. I usually hang out close by or over by the river. I am an excellent actor and I love to play dead when there's danger around. I fooled you, didn't I?"

"Not really. I was getting ready to squish you with one paw to make sure. Anyway, I'm glad you're not dead. I could use a friend right now. So how about we get something to eat? I'm starving. Oh, by the way, my friends call me Max."

"Well, you're just in time. I am just on my way out to dinner. I eat out every night. So far, I've got some slugs and snails, some berries and a frog or two. Maybe I'll get a few cockroaches for dessert," Mr. O. explained.

Max gulped. "Thanks, anyway, Mr. O. I'll pass for now. I'm more of a hamburger kind of guy, myself. What else do you do besides roam around all night?" Max asked, trying to change the subject. "Nothing much, pretending is my main job. I'm really good at it. How about you? Aren't you pretending you're not lost?"

"I can't be. I'm a great Schnauzer. I always know where I'm going and never get lost. If you don't mind, I'll just stretch my paws out and think about it for a while," Max confided.

"Just pretend you're dead like me until I get back. Remember, though, no breakfast. I eat out all the time," Mr. O. said, as he scurried away into the woods.

When he returned the next morning, he had several other creatures with him. "Hey, Mr. Max. I brought a couple of friends home to meet you. I think they might be able to help you out. They are a lot better with directions than I am. I have to get going now, it's my bedtime. Nice to meet ya," Mr. O. called out, as he disappeared into the tall grass.

"Hello, Mr. Max. I'm Emilio, that's short for Armadillo. This is my lovely friend, Izabella, one of my favorite girl lizards," Emilio said.

Max sniffed the two creatures. "Hello, guys. I have a lot of lizard friends back where I used to live, but I've never met an Armadillo.

Izabella spoke up first, "He's not so good looking, but he can sniff out lots of food with his big snout. Together, we can catch a great spread of mosquitoes, gnats, and juicy flies. Do you want to come with us? We'll help you find something to eat," she asked.

"Thanks, but I was thinking more along the lines of a juicy hamburger and it's time I got going. I'm trying to find the yellow school bus. Do you ever see the yellow bus?" Max asked.

Izabella wiggled, excitedly, "I know! I know where it goes. Follow that road. The one next to the railroad tracks, over there. That's where it goes."

"That's the best news ever! Thank you," Max called out, as he leaped out of the bushes and ran toward the railroad tracks.

5.

GIANT JACK RABBIT

Max walked along the road for many miles. He was so hungry, he almost wished he had Izabella's bugs. Convinced he smelled a river nearby, he left the road, crossed the railroad tracks, and entered the woods.

When he came to the edge of a steep cliff, he discovered the river bed below. Maximilian T. McKnight, a city dog, was no more. For the first time in his life, he was totally alone and fighting for survival. He knew he had to have water and find a safe way down the cliff. He started going down, one paw at a time. When he stumbled and lost his footing, he would slide or roll until he got to a safer place.

When he finally reached the bottom, he dunked himself several times, then, stood in the cold water to soothe his wounds and burning paws. He drank as much water as he could, shook himself off, and lay down on the soft sand.

Max thought about his new friend, Mr. O., but did not pretend he was dead. Instead, he pretended he was swinging in his hammock and Ma and Pa were close by. Just as he was drifting off to sleep, something jumped out and began racing back and forth in front of him. *Wow, that thing's big, and fast, too. Maybe it's a small deer or even a kangaroo. No, that can't be. Those are the biggest ears I've ever seen. I'll speak up first and catch it off guard.*

"Kind of jumpy aren't you? Max asked." Can't you stand still for two seconds, so I can see you? Who are you, anyway?"

"What do you mean?" the thing answered. "Who are you?"

"I am Max, giant of all Schnauzer dogs."

"Ya? Well, I'm Jack, the giant of all Jackrabbits. I'm not one of those little white and pink sissy bunnies. Actually, I'm not a rabbit at all. I'm one of the world's largest hares. I can outrun you or any dog, kick-box with my back legs, and hop over ten feet at a time. So you better not mess with me."

"You can't outrun all dogs. There is one dog I know of, for sure. He lived close by, so I knew him pretty well. Bet you don't even know what kind it is," Max challenged him.

"Okay, so the big greyhound dog is one exception, big deal. If I got paid to be a racer, I would be in first place at the finish line, too. And, who else has giant ears to keep him warm and provide superior hearing? Nobody has ears as great as mine," the Jackrabbit bragged on.

"I agree. I don't have giant ears and I can't hop, but we do have some things in common. We're both giants and we're both fast runners," Max told him.

"You are totally right! We're also very smart and good looking. Hey, we're more alike than we are different. How about that? Let's be friends. I'll call you Max and you can call me Jack. Follow me, my new giant friend," Jack called out, as he took giant leaps into the air and hopped away.

Even though Max could run like a racer, it was difficult for him to keep up with Jack. When he suddenly disappeared, Max stopped up short. "Hey, over here," Jack called out of the bushes. Max ran toward Jack and leaped right into a shallow underground pit covered in shrubs and clumps of grass.

When his eyes adjusted, he could see there were bunches of grass, flowering plants, stacks of twigs and carrots hanging from the grass roof. What was even better, Jack kept a pretty, cool supply of groceries.

"I don't stock steaks or burgers, but how's about a nifty salad?" Jack offered. "I've got lots of lettuce and carrots."

Max could not believe his ears. He would happily eat carrots all day instead of bugs. "Thank you, Jack. You have made a really, nice home here. I couldn't have found another giant more kind and generous than you," Max said, gratefully.

"Do you know what, Max? I can lie on my back, put my ears back, and hide here all day long. If I go out in daylight, everything is chasing after me. Coyotes, hawks, and even hunters think I would make a really tasty lunch. So, I go out looking for food every night and come back here in the morning and hide until the next night. But what are you doing way out here? Are you looking for something?" Jack asked.

"I've got to find the big, yellow school bus. I was guarding someone very important and I can't find him anywhere. I've been looking for days now," Max told him.

"I know a lot of folks but it sounds like you need to talk with somebody who's really wise," Jack told him

"What about that bird that's supposed to be so wise?" Max asked.

"You mean the old Horned Owl? I wasn't thinking of him, exactly," Jack answered. "He's been after me for years. There is one in particular, though, that might help us out. We'll have to travel undercover for a long way and take off right before dark. It's pretty far across a big field and into a forest of trees. You'll have to keep up with me, so don't stop to do any of that sniffing around and stuff. Timing is everything."

6

MRS. SNOWY OWL

It was early evening when Jack whispered, "Let's go see if we can find us some owls." They slowly climbed out of the grass house and ran along the river until they reached a large field. When the night sky was almost black, they maneuvered their way across the field and into the dense woods on the other side. They hid in the woods for several hours until they heard owl-like sounds filtering down through the tall trees.

Jack cautioned Max, "We have to listen very carefully. I've got to be sure it's not the Great Horned Owl. He makes two short hoots and one long one." They waited in silence for quite a while, then, they heard a different owl sound, "Hoooo's looking for owls, the wisest of all birds?"

Jack whispered, "It's her, the one I'm looking for. Look up, you'll see her." Max scanned over the trees until he could make out a beautiful, white, snowy owl. "How is a dog like me supposed to talk to an owl?" he whispered. "

"We don't need to know. She's strange but very kind," Jack whispered.

"It's me, the giant jackrabbit, Mrs. Owl. Remember me?" Jack asked.

"My, hooooow you've changed. You've turned into a black giant. How clever of you to disguise yourself," she answered.

"Perhaps you may be squinting, dear Mrs. Owl. This is my friend, Max, Manhattan Max. I'm still the same beautiful giant I always was," Jack answered.

"Oooooh, I see. Why is a city dog looking for a yellow school bus? Hooooow strange," Mrs. Owl asked.

Max stepped up and spoke to her, "I'm honored to meet you, Mrs. Owl. I have lost my dear young friend. Can you help me find the yellow school bus?"

"Ooooooh dear, a young child," she answered. "Because I am the wisest, I hear all. While they do spill and get dirty, you must promise to always be friendly to all the children. Remember, I will hear. 'Girlie' girls, Mr. Max, are a precious gift. I am the 'girliest,' girl of all. Do you understand? Then, think hard. Hooooo is it that you truly love as much as Ma and Pa?" Mrs. Owl asked.

"I really do understand, Mrs. Owl. I don't think that way anymore. I love Billy and little Wyatt, and Sophie, too," Max answered.

"And Hooooo else?"

"All children everywhere," Max added.

"While I am the wisest, the Hawk flies the highest and sees all."

"Can I meet the great Hawk?" Max asked.

"He does not come often, but I will tempt him with a plump, gray mouse. If you wait, giant Schnauzer, he will come and steal my dinner. Remember, wait and watch, goooooodbye."

"Oh, thank you, most beautiful, Mrs. Owl. Jack and I are ever so grateful." Oh, no, no! Not me. I've got to be gone, real gone. That mouse isn't all that hawk will steal. Do you know what he will do with a fat rabbit like me? Sorry, my friend, look me up when you're in the neighborhood. Gotta run, gotta run," Jack called out as he hopped out of sight.

Much later in the silence of the night, the plump grey mouse fell to the ground with a soft thud. Mrs. Owl had kept her promise.

7

THE GREAT HAWK

Max stayed in place and stared at the gray mouse for a long time. When it was just about light, a huge, dark shadow hovered in the sky above him. He lay very still and prayed the great Hawk would not want him for dinner, too. Before he could open his eyes, the hawk swooped down, snatched the mouse and ascended back toward the sky. "Excuse me, please come back," Max called out. "Mrs. Owl sent me. She said you have excellent eyesight."

"Mrs. Owl is very wise, indeed," the hawk called back. "Go back to the field at the edge of the forest. I will return."

Once again, Max embarked on a new journey and set out to meet the great hawk. It was a long walk back to the field, but he was determined not to give up. As he got closer to the edge of the forest, he could see the hawk descending from the sky. His giant wings cast a huge shadow over Max.

"How do you think I can help you?" his deep voice echoed down.

"I've lost my little friend and I must find the yellow school bus," Max explained

"The city has many yellow buses. Are you a city dog?"

"Yes, I am Manhattan Max, a city dog."

"I cannot help you, then."

"No, no wait. I'm not a city dog anymore," Max pleaded.

The great hawk peered down at Max. "Then, you must turn around. You have come too far. Close your eyes, and listen for your master. What does he say?"

Max lay down in his thinking position, stretched his front paws out in front and covered his ears to listen. Out of nowhere, he began to hear Pa's voice. "If you're ever lost or in danger, follow the river. Follow the river, Max, until you find your way home."

When Max looked up, the great hawk was circling high in the sky. He barked as loud as he could. "I hear him. I hear Pa. Thank you, I will find my way."

Max fought his way through bushes and dense trees until he reached the river, and finally, the main road. He ran hard at first, then, he walked, and ran again. When he sensed he might be getting close, he thought of Jack and started running as fast as he could.

He could see the school bus sign off in the distance, and a small group of people standing close by. They were calling his name and cheering him on. His eyes quickly scanned the group, searching for one face, and one face, only.

Suddenly, Ma's arms were around his neck, "Oh, Max, I just knew. You went looking for Billy, didn't you? Shame on us, we forgot again."

Max rested his head on Ma's shoulder and looked up. He saw Pa, little Wyatt, Sophie, and a little girl he didn't know or did he? One sniff and he knew it was Billy.

I wonder why Ma is dressing him up like a girl. He can't wrestle and tumble around wearing a dress and a pink hat. Wait a minute, Ma wouldn't do that, unless, unless Billy really is a girl. Oh, wow, that's why Mrs. Owl was talking about me and 'girlie' girls. She knew Billy is a girl. How about that, a real 'girlie,' girl, just like Mrs. Owl!

Max was, over the moon, happy to see Billy. If she looked like Izabella, he wouldn't have cared one bit. He knew he would never make fun of little girls again.

When Ma and Billy finally let go of Max, Pa came and bent over him. "You're a number one detective and guard dog, Max. I don't know what this family would do without you. Let's make a deal. We're never going to go on another trip without you, and don't you ever take off on another trip without us." Pa shook Max's paw and everyone laughed.

Maximilian T. McKnight, also known as Manhattan Max, would never be the same. His jeweled collar was gone, his coat was shabby, his toenails were ragged and he was covered in dead grass.

None of it mattered. He was just Max. A new Max who had many new friends and loved all kids, everywhere, especially the one with soft pink cheeks and long braids, a girl named Billy. Max, a family dog, was finally home.

The End

Made in the USA
Lexington, KY
16 December 2019